CW00840101

First Printing, 2020
Published Independently

ISBN : 9798553269586

Illustrations by Shutterstock

Greenhouse Adventures is a series of seven stories :

The Cactus

The Grapevine

Lotties Very Bad Day

Colins New Friend

The Stormy Day

The Sunflower

Where Is Mr Thompson ?

Colins New Friend

Colins New Friend

It was a normal day in the greenhouse. Mr Thompson had been moving some pots around on the middle shelf while making quite a lot of noise.

Thankfully, when he had left, this time he closed the door.

''What's he been doing all day?" asked Polly looking up at the middle shelf.

''I'm not sure" jumped up Colin, but I am going to find out "

''Oh my" Bertie said, hoping that no one would be leaving the ground floor. He much preferred it when everyone stayed where they were all supposed to be.

"I won't be long " said Colin, starting to climb already. He had had a good sleep and was in the mood to have an adventure, as long as it was a good one.

Polly left her soil and went over to Cara '' He's so brave "she sighed, wondering what he would find.

Lottie looked at her leaves making sure they were okay and hadn't been nibbled on anymore.

''Are you ok Lottie?" asked Peter noticing her checking all of her leaves.

"Yes I am today thank you" she answered really hoping that she would never see Sally the slug again.

Suddenly the fruit and vegetables heard Colin laughing and chatting but couldn't hear what he was saying.

''What is he doing up there?" Lottie snapped, wondering once again why he was away from them for so long and why he wasn't telling them anything.

"Oh Colin please come back down" said Bertie longing for his friend to come back to the ground floor.

Colin poked his head over the shelf and was beaming a big smile.

''I'm ok everyone'' he smiled. ''I'm having a great time''

''What's up there?'' Polly asked but Colin didn't answer her, he was having a great time with a new friend he had just made.

Colin had found a pot of soil with a big red round tomato sitting in it. He had introduced himself as Tommy and they were having a great time laughing and joking and exchanging stories.

Colin knew that him and Tommy were going to be friends for a very long time. He didn't know why but he felt like he had a great connection with him. Maybe cucumbers and tomatoes were just grown to be friends.

All the other produce were getting annoyed with Colin for taking so long and all they could hear was his laughter.

''What's taking him so long to come back down?" Peter said, missing his friend.

After what seemed like hours later, Colin started to make his way back. When he jumped down from the middle shelf, he was still laughing to himself and went back to his soil.

"All that laughing has made me tired" He said, closing his eyes.

''So, aren't you going to tell us what's in the new pot?" Cara asked but Colin was already laying down and was fast asleep.

"He didn't even say goodnight "snapped Lottie secretly wishing she had had some fun too.

''Well I'm just pleased he's back safe and sound" said Bertie happy that everyone was where they should be and now he could have a good nights sleep without having to cover his eyes or his ears. He was finding it very hard to sleep while doing that!
"We will just have to wait until tomorrow to find out what he found "said Polly, sounding very disappointed.
''I don't even want to know now" snapped Lottie, very annoyed with her friend. Colin always had an adventure, but he would always tell them all about it. Never before had he not told them and then gone to sleep without saying goodnight. Lottie was disgusted.
Polly and Cara started to get comfortable for their nights sleep, both feeling disappointed with their friend.

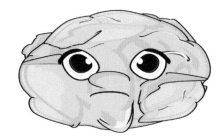

Everyone was quiet, no one said a word and then soon they were all sound asleep.

The next morning, they all awoke to the sound of Mr Thompson opening the greenhouse door and pottering around. They watched as he looked at all his produce. He would move pots around and occasionally nod or shake his head. He looked up at the grapevine which had grown a lot and now had many more leaves. Even the tiny green balls had grown a lot. Mr Thompson nodded when he looked at this.

Colin watched as he started to move things around on the middle shelf. He did hope that Tommy was ok. He had made friends with him yesterday and was looking forward to spending more time with him today. Tommy was a big red round ball of fun. Colin smiled to himself at the thought of seeing him later and as he turned his head, he noticed that the other produce were all looking at him. He smiled but they didn't seem to have seen him as they didn't smile back. He just wanted Mr Thompson to leave soon so he could go and visit Tommy.

Normally he wasn't too keen to go climbing unless he really had to, but today he couldn't wait.

Mr Thompson was a long time doing something on the middle shelf and he kept muttering to himself.

Finally, he decided it was time to leave for the day and left the greenhouse, closing the door behind him. Lottie was just about to ask Colin what he had been doing yesterday, when he jumped out of his soil and started to make his way to the middle shelf.

''I need to make sure Tommy's alright" he said climbing his way up on the shelf. The other fruit and vegetables looked In dismay as he had left them again.

Cara and Polly looked sad as they watched him disappear.

"Oh my, I wish he would just stay on the ground floor" Bertie said, already starting to worry.

Colin had gone straight to Tommy and was already laughing and having fun with his new friend.

''He has never left us like that before" said Polly, feeling very upset.
''I KNOW'' Lottie snapped.
''We will just have to wait until he comes back down" Peter said, also feeling very disappointed and very left out.
''I am not going to let him go to sleep without saying goodnight again" said Lottie "That was very mean of him"
Polly had forgotten about that until Lottie reminded her. They had never gone to sleep before without saying it and she suddenly felt very sad.

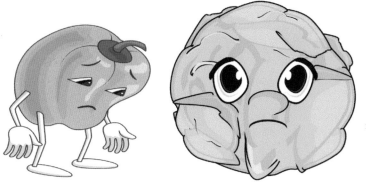

Cara also thought about how they had all fallen asleep without speaking. That was very strange. Lottie realised that she still didn't know what or who Colin had found but she did know that whatever it was, she didn't like it.

They all stayed very quiet on the ground floor as they didn't feel like talking. Cara didn't even leave her soil which was very unusual for her. Today she just didn't feel like it.

The produce still quiet, noticed that it was starting to get dark and Colin was still above them on the middle shelf.

After a while, they all watched as he started to make his way down.

''That guy is such a character" he smiled, chuckling to himself as he made his way back to his soil. He looked around at the others who were just looking at him with blank faces.

"What's wrong?" He asked, wondering why they didn't look very happy.

''What is on the middle shelf?"

''And what was so funny?"

''And why were you up there so long?" asked Lottie, angrily.

"And why didn't you say goodnight to us last night?" Cara asked him. Colin thought back on his actions the night before and remembered that he hadn't told his friends who he had met and much worse, he had fallen asleep without talking to them and without wishing them a goodnight.

Colin felt ashamed of himself and jumped back out of his pot.

"Oh I am so sorry please forgive me" His friends were all looking at him still not smiling.

"I guess I got so caught up with meeting Tommy that I forgot to spend time with you all. I am really really sorry" He was hoping that they would say something, but they were all still silent. This was going to be a lot harder than he thought.

"Who is Tommy?" Peter asked finally breaking the silence.

Colin was happy that his potato friend was talking to him again.

"He is a very funny red tomato" said Colin, hoping that everyone else would speak to him too.

"Like when Peter came and he introduced himself and we all had a lot of fun and spent a lot of time getting to know him" said Cara, trying to make a point.

Colin remembered how they had all wondered what was in the pot that Mr Thompson had left on the ground floor and how they had all enjoyed meeting him. "Yes, you are right Cara that was a very good day"

Colin felt really bad that he had left all of his friends out while trying to get to know his new friend Tommy.

"I do feel really bad you are all my best friends and I really don't want you to feel sad"

Cara gave him a big smile.

''Next time please make sure you tell us all about your adventure" Added Polly.

''Yes, and saying goodnight would be good" Lottie grumbled.

''You've got it" Colin laughed "and again, I really am sorry"

For the rest of the evening, the friends were laughing and talking normally again until they started to get tired. Colin layed down and started to yawn.

''Goodnight everyone" He said, happy that they were all friends again. Bertie was happy that everyone was talking, and everything was good and yet again, he didn't have to cover his eyes or his ears.

''Goodnight" They all answered, also happy that they had their friend back.

"Goodnight" came a voice from the top shelf.

THE

STORMY

DAY

The Stormy Day

Mr Thompson was doing his daily routine in the greenhouse while all the fruit and vegetables were watching him.

Colin could see he was looking at his friend Tommy the tomato. He didn't like to talk about Tommy much to his friends after they had been upset with him for leaving them out. Colin still felt really bad for that and had been trying to make it up to them ever since.

He did feel a bit sad that he hadn't seen Tommy since that day and hoped that he was having a good time with the other tomato plants on the middle shelf.

As Mr Thompson was about to leave, Colin noticed that he was carrying some pots including the one with Tommy. Once he had left the greenhouse, everyone turned to Colin. He wondered why they were all looking at him.

''Colin, your friend has gone'' said Cara, looking a bit sad. Colin looked over at the door and then back at Cara.

"It's fine" He smiled, trying to put on a brave face.
Deep down he was feeling disappointed that Mr Thompson had taken away his friend and was also feeling a bit guilty for not spending much time with him lately.
"I'm sure Tommy will be very happy outside with his new friends" He hoped he was right.
While the fruit and vegetables were talking, suddenly there was a loud bang.
"Oh my, what was that?" Asked Bertie the Brussel, covering his ears.
At that moment there was another loud bang and then a bright light filled the greenhouse.
"Don't worry everyone, its just a storm"
said Colin looking over to check on Bertie
but he couldn't see him.

Colin had been in the greenhouse for a very long time, much longer than the others and had seen and heard a few storms.
''Where's Bertie?" He asked.
Cara and Polly were hugging each other looking quite frightened.
''I'm here" said a voice although nobody could see him.
''Bertie where are you?" Lottie asked, getting worried.
''I'm hiding from the horrible noise" came a voice.
Just then another loud bang and a flash of light appeared, and Bertie came running out from behind Peter the Potato's pot.
''Oh my, oh my it's too loud" he shrieked, not knowing where to run to.
''Come over here" smiled Lottie, opening her leaves for him to hide under. He ran and took cover.

"Don't panic everyone it's just the weather" Colin tried to explain.

"It's very loud" Polly said, still hugging Cara.

Peter moved slowly out of his pot. "Colin's right, it's just a storm, we are safe inside and are lucky that we are not out in the garden"

Colin remembered that Mr Thompson had taken Tommy outside and really hoped that he was okay. He walked over to the door and could see Tommy standing up in some soil outside of the greenhouse. He seemed to be swaying slightly.

"It looks windy out there" Colin told the others, feeling sorry for Tommy who was now out in the cold, wet weather.

Suddenly it sounded like large stones were hitting the greenhouse.

"Oh my" Lottie could hear Bertie underneath her leaves.

"You're safe here" she assured him.

''It's just the rain hitting against the windows hopefully it will stop soon"
Colin was trying to reassure his friends.

''I hope so or we won't get any sleep tonight" said Cara, sounding
worried.

''Yes, we may be in for a very long night if this storm doesn't stop soon"
Peter said, hoping it would.

Colin was looking up onto the top shelf. He was wondering if Curtis
was okay. He had told Colin that he needed sunlight and Colin was
hoping that the storm wasn't upsetting Curtis
too much.

Lottie was watching Colin and could tell that he
was planning something.

''We need you down here" she said sternly,
hoping he wasn't going to leave her to look
after everyone by herself.

''I'm a bit worried about Curtis" He answered.

"But he is up on the top shelf, you can't do anything while this storm is going on"

''I think I should go and check on him"

''Oh my" came a sound from Lottie's leaves.

''Why don't you shout up to him?" Polly suggested, hoping that would work instead. She felt safer when Colin was nearby.

''He won't be able to hear me with the rain hitting against the windows, no I'm going to go and check on him. Don't worry I'll be straight back."

Peter, Polly, Cara and Lottie all looked at one another, they all knew that Colin was never quick when he went anywhere but they kept quiet. Colin knew it was quite risky climbing up to the top shelf, especially when the storm was so loud. He would have to be brave and attempt it.

''Oh, please hurry" Cara said, knowing that nobody would be able to talk him out of it.

Lottie could feel Bertie quivering even more underneath her.

Colin started to climb up onto the middle shelf. He was getting quite an expert at climbing now. When he got there, he looked at the empty spaces where his friend Tommy and the other tomato plants had been. He was nearer to the window now and could hear the heavy rain even more. It was definitely scarier up here on the shelf.

Colin could see Tommy from the window. He was still swaying and looked very wet. He wished that Tommy had stayed inside and would be dry now.

Colin remembered why he was there, he still had to climb up to the shelf above him and check on Curtis. He started to climb up and as he reached the top shelf, he saw Curtis looking slightly worried.

''Colin'' He smiled when he saw him.

''I just wanted to check you are alright''
Colin smiled back, glad that his friend was pleased to see him.

"I'm not used to this loud noise and I'm not too keen on the bright lights" Curtis told him.

"It's just a storm you re safe inside "

Curtis was happy to see Colin he hadn't seen him for a while.

"You're looking well" Colin said, trying to take his mind off the storm.

They both chatted for a while. Suddenly there was a light shining through the window.

"The suns coming out" said Colin, happily. "I 'd better go back down to the others. "

Colin remembered the last time he was on an adventure and that he had been gone too long, his friends weren't very happy with him.

"Thank you for coming to check on me"

Curtis said looking a lot happier now that the rain had stopped.

"It was great to see you again"

Colin turned to go back down. He was pleased it wouldn't be so noisy climbing down. When he stood on the middle shelf, he thought about Tommy again. Now it was sunny, he hoped his friend would get dry. Colin had an idea while he was standing on the middle shelf, he would check on his friend. He walked over to the window and looked down to the ground where Tommy was now. As he looked out, Tommy was looking up at the window and smiled.

Colin was so happy to see his friend and waved. Tommy gave a big wave back. Colin now knew that Tommy was not angry with him for not seeing him lately. This made him very happy. He waved one more time and then made his way to the ground floor.

"Is Curtis ok?" asked Cara as soon as she saw him.

"Yes, he is now that the storm has stopped"

Colin noticed that Bertie was now back in his usual spot and looked happy again. Cara and Polly had stopped hugging now too.

Colin went and laid on his soil and was feeling pleased with himself. He was pleased he had checked on Curtis after all.

"I'm so pleased the storm is over we can have a good nights sleep now." Said Peter, settling down into his earth.

The friends chatted about the storm until it got dark again.

Colin was secretly happy that the storm had happened. If it hadn't, he wouldn't have seen his friend Curtis and wouldn't have been able to wave to his good friend Tommy. This made him very happy.

"Goodnight everyone" Colin yawned.

"Goodnight" they all replied

"Goodnight" came a voice from the top shelf.

The Sunflower

The Sunflower

Mr Thompson was in his greenhouse. He had put a pot in the corner on the ground and was admiring it. After watering some of his produce, he decided to leave, closing the door behind him. Lottie sighed with relief. She was so happy that she hadn't been watered. Colin and the others were all standing around the new pot. Lottie jumped out of her soil and joined them. In the middle of it was a very bright yellow flower. It had a very tall stem.

''WOW" said Bertie feeling very small next to the very tall flower.

''It's very bright" Polly smiled, while squinting her eyes.

The sunflower bowed down its head and looked at all the small fruit and vegetables standing around its pot.

''Can I help you?" It asked.

''We are admiring you" smiled Cara. ''We havn't seen anything like you before"

"Well thank you" the flower replied.
"You look like a big bright sun" Polly beamed.
The flower laughed.
"My dear, I am meant to look like the sun. I am a sunflower" she explained.
"Wow" said Bertie again.
"You are very tall" added Lottie.

Colin was studying the new addition to the greenhouse. Polly was right, it was like they had their own sunshine.
"Have you got a name?" asked Colin.
"You can call me Sunny" replied the sunflower.
"And who are you?"
Everyone introduced themselves. They all liked having Sunny there, she brightened up the place.
While the produce were chatting with Sunny, Bertie started to whimper. "Oh my oh my"
"What's the matter Bertie?" Colin asked him.
"There's something making a funny noise"
He answered.

They all stopped talking to see what Bertie had heard. Colin could hear it too.
"BUZZZZZZZZZZZZZZZZZZZZZZZZZZZZZZZZZZZZZZZZZZZZZ"
There was a creature flying around Sunny and it was making an awful sound.

"Where did you come from?" Colin asked as it flew around. "Through the window of course" buzzed the creature, still flying around. Everyone looked up towards the window and it was right, Mr Thompson had left the window open.

"Oh my" said Bertie, remembering what had happened when the door had been left open recently.

"Oh no not again, I don't want anything coming in and nibbling at me again" said Lottie. She still hadn't got over the trauma of meeting Sally the slug. She still shivered now thinking about it.

Colin and Peter were looking at eachother also hoping that nothing else would fly into the greenhouse.

"Will you please stop flying around me making that awful noise?" moaned Sunny.

"But you smell so sweet" It replied, landing on the top of Sunnys head. "I am a bumble bee. I am supposed to annoy flowers, especially bright yellow ones that smell so good"

Colin was looking at how angry Sunny was getting and started to think how he could get rid of the bumble bee. He was annoyed that Mr Thompson had left the window open.

"BUZZZZZZZZZZZZZZZZZZZZZZZZZZZZZZZZZZZZZZZZZZZZZZZ"

"Oh my, oh my" said Bertie, not liking the noise that the bee was making and decided to cover his ears. It had been a while since he had needed to do that.

Colin decided to be brave and talk to the bee calmly. "Please bumble bee, would you mind leaving our friend alone"

"Yes, please do" said Sunny, I just want to stand here peacefully and grow my beautiful petals"

"I'm very sorry" buzzed the bee "But I am trying to get some pollen from you to make some honey"

"I don't like the sound of that at all" said Lottie.

"It's what bees do" buzzed the bee.

Colin had an idea.

"If you were to go back out of the window, you will see lots of lovely flowers where you can get your pollen"

"Oh yes" said Cara, feeling happy that the bee would soon leave and she wouldn't have to put up with that buzzing noise for much longer. She looked over at Bertie who was still covering his ears and she didn't blame him.

"Then maybe I will" buzzed the bee, flying up towards the window. They all watched as it flew out.

"Hurrah" They all shouted. Bertie saw that the bee had left and took his hands away from his ears.

"That's better" He smiled.
"Oh thank you so much Colin" Sunny smiled. She was so much
happier now that the noisy bee had gone away.
"You are a very pretty flower" said Peter, trying not to blush.
Everyone laughed. Colin was pleased with himself for getting the bee
to leave but then he had a horrible thought. He had told it to go into
the garden to the other flowers but
that was where his friend Tommy was.
He hoped that it wouldn't bother
him and the other tomato plants.

A shadow came over the roof of the greenhouse and Colin knew that meant that the sun was setting. The produce all went back to their normal places apart from Sunny who was still in her pot.

"I'm really glad you're here Sunny" smiled Colin as he started to yawn. It had been a very tiring day.

"Thank you and thank you again for saving me from that annoying bee. I want my pollen all to myself" Sunny smiled back. While Colin was laying down, he saw the window and realised it was still open. He thought it best not to mention it to the others as he didn't want to worry them and the last thing he wanted was to have a sleepless night like last time.

I'm sure it'll be fine he thought, although he remembered that Curtis was up next to the window and hoped that he would be okay.

"It's been an exhausting day" Cara sighed as she closed her eyes.

"It's been a very noisy one" said Bertie. Everyone laughed.

"Goodnight" Colin sighed.

"Goodnight" They all replied, even Sunny joined in.

"Goodnight" came a voice from the top shelf.

Look Out For Greenhouse Adventures Book 3 Coming Soon:

Where Is Mr Thompson ?

The New Arrival

The Magical Tree

GREENHOUSE ADVENTURES

Written By
KAREN DONNA

Printed in Great Britain
by Amazon